Aunt Ant Leaves through the Leaves

A Story with Homophones and Homonyms

by NANCY COFFELT

Holiday House / New York

Ant squints an **eye**.

"Not **I**. I'm a new **aunt**, and it's after **two**. I have a new niece I need **to** get to!"

And Aunt Ant **leaves** through the **leaves**.

Monkey says, "**Bee, hi! Be** a friend and help me. This pile's too **high!**"

Bee squints an eye. "Not I. I have too many things to **do**, and this week's shipment of honey is **due**."

And Bee leaves through the leaves.

"Oh, **Bear**, this is more than I can **bear**. **Wait**! Will you help me pull this **weight**?"

Bear squints an eye.

"Not I. See that **fir**? It got sap all over my **fur**."

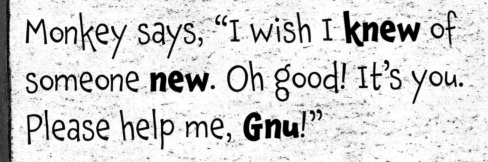

Monkey says, "I wish I **knew** of someone **new**. Oh good! It's you. Please help me, **Gnu!**"

Gnu squints an eye.

"Not I! If I were **you**,
                    I'd ask **Ewe**."

And Gnu leaves through the leaves.

"Aunt Ant! You came back!"

Monkey grabs a **pail**.

Monkey and ants work until the sky grows **pale**.

Monkey says, "You really are a helpful **lot**. All of you have helped a **lot**."

Later . . .

"**Whose** job will it be to move the peels off my porch?" Monkey asks. "**Who's** going to help me now?"

"I will!" says Bee.

"I will!" says Bear.

"I will!" say Gnu and Ewe and Deer.

Then the animals call, "Monkey, look. See! We care! And **they're** easy to move from here to **there**. Now may we have a pie that's **ours**? We've been working for a couple of **hours**."

"Here you **go**! And I must **go**. Aunt Ant wants me to meet her niece. Enjoy your **piece** of pie in **peace**."

And Monkey leaves, er, waddles through the leaves.

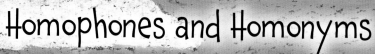

Homophones and Homonyms

"One/won," "deer/dear," "there/their/they're." What are these words? Homophones! Homophones are words that sound the same but have different spellings and mean entirely different things.

Sometimes homophones aren't what they seem. People pronounce some words differently in different parts of the country. For example, for some people, "our" and "hour" are homophones. For others, "our" and "are" are homophones.

And what about the word "aunt"? Some people pronounce "aunt" so it rhymes with "pant." Then "aunt" and "ant" are homophones. But other people pronounce "aunt" so it rhymes with "haunt."

In the strict sense, homonyms sound the same and are spelled the same, as in "bark" and "bark." Your dog can bark, and a tree is covered in bark.

And sometimes the word "homonym" is used to describe either homophones or homonyms.

What's a poor monkey to do?

Practice his homonyms and homophones!

To my Rockin' Writer Girls and the fabulous
3rd-grade classes of Jackson School

Library of Congress Cataloging-in-Publication Data
Coffelt, Nancy.
Aunt Ant leaves through the leaves : a story with homophones and homonyms / by Nancy Coffelt. — 1st ed.
p. cm.
Summary: In a homonym-filled tale reminiscent of "The little red hen," a monkey asks for help
moving a stack of bananas so that he can bake a pie.
ISBN 978-0-8234-2353-8 (hardcover)
[1. Helpfulness—Fiction. 2. Animals—Fiction. 3. English language—Homonyms.] I. Title.
PZ7.C658Aun 2011
[E]—dc22
2010030737